KT-199-122

This Topsy and Tim
book belongs to

_____

Topsy + Tim

meet the firefighters

Jean and Gareth Adamson

All Ladybird books are available at most bookshops, supermarkets
and newsagents, or can be ordered direct from:
Ladybird Postal Sales PO Box 133 Paignton TQ3 2YP England
Telephone: (+44) 01803 554761   *Fax:* (+44) 01803 663394
A catalogue record for this book is available from the British Library

Published by Ladybird Books Ltd
A subsidiary of the Penguin Group
A Pearson Company

© Jean and Gareth Adamson MCMXCV
This edition MCMXCVIII

The moral rights of the author/illustrator have been asserted
LADYBIRD and the device of a Ladybird are trademarks of Ladybird Books Ltd Loughborough Leicestershire UK

*All rights reserved. No part of this publication may be reproduced, stored in a retrieval system, or transmitted in any form or
by any means, electronic, mechanical, photocopying, recording or otherwise, without the prior consent of the copyright owner.*

One morning when Topsy and Tim
were on their way to school, they
heard a fire engine coming.

It raced past them, sirens sounding
and blue lights flashing. All the
other traffic got out of the way.
Everyone knew that the firefighters
were hurrying to put out a fire.

'Kerry's dad is a firefighter,' said
Topsy. 'I expect he is on that fire
engine.'

But Kerry's dad was not on the
fire engine. It was his morning
off and he was taking Kerry to
school. Topsy and Tim told him
about the fire engine they had seen.
'They're called fire appliances, not
fire engines,' said Kerry.

'There's an open day at my
fire station on Saturday,' said
Kerry's dad. 'Would you like to
come and see all our fire appliances?'
'Yes, please,' said Topsy and Tim.
On Saturday Topsy and Tim
and Mummy set out for
Bellford Fire Station.

There were lots of children at
the fire station. Firefighters in
yellow helmets were looking after
them. Topsy and Tim soon found
Kerry and her dad.

Kerry was waiting to go up on
a long turntable ladder. Topsy
and Tim wanted to go up too.
A firefighter helped them all
into a cage on the end of
the ladder. He gave them
safety helmets to wear.

A firefighter at the
back of the appliance
pulled a lever and the
ladder started to go up.

It grew longer and longer and
went higher and higher, until
the people on the ground looked
as small as toys.
'We hose water down on to burning
buildings from up here,' said
the firefighter.
'And you rescue people from high
windows and roofs,' said Kerry.

When they came down from the ladder
Mummy bought them each a little
firefighter's helmet.
'I'm going to be a firefighter
when I grow up,' said Kerry.
'Can girls be firefighters?' asked Topsy.
'I don't think so,' said Tim.

'Yes, they can!' said the lady
who was selling the toy helmets.
'I'm a firefighter, just like Kerry's
dad. Women can be firefighters, but
they have to be as strong and as
brave as the men.'
To show how strong she was, she gave
Tim a fireman's lift.

Kerry's dad took them to see
how the fire station worked.
'When there is a fire and someone
phones 999,' he said, 'we get
the message on a teleprinter.
A loudspeaker tells us where to go
and which appliances to take.'

'Alarm bells ring and the firefighters
run to the appliances. If they are
upstairs they slide down a pole.
It's quicker than running down the
stairs.'

Kerry's dad lifted the children
into the cab of a big fire appliance.
They pretended to drive to a fire.

Near the big fire appliance
was a much smaller one.
'Is that a baby fire engine?'
asked Tim.
'It's a van full of rescue equipment,'
said Kerry's dad. 'We take it to
accidents and rescue people from
crashed cars and trucks.'

Kerry's dad showed them the tall
tower where the firefighters practised
with their ladders and hoses.
'When we have finished we hang
the hoses in the tower to dry,'
he told them.

Next to the tower was a room
that had been on fire. It made
their noses tickle.
'We make smoky fires in there,'
said Kerry's dad. 'Then we practise
putting them out and rescuing people.
We have to wear masks and carry tanks
of air on our backs, or we would choke.'

Kerry took Topsy and Tim into
a showroom full of
fire dangers. It looked like
an ordinary living room.
'See if you can spot where
fires could start,' said Kerry.
Tim spotted a cigarette on an
armchair seat.
'That could start a fire,' he said.

Topsy spotted a box of matches
on the floor.
'A naughty little child might start
a fire with those,' she said.
'And that electric heater should
be behind a fireguard,' said Mummy.

Mummy spotted more fire dangers
near a kitchen stove.
'Are smoke-detectors any use?'
she asked Kerry's dad. 'I think
I ought to get one.'

Kerry's dad showed them a smoke-
detector and made it work. It
made loud BLEEP-BLEEP-BLEEP noises.
'If there was a fire in your home
one night, the smoke-detector
would wake you up,' he said.
'We've got one,' Kerry told Topsy.

It was time to go home, but
before they went, Kerry's dad
gave them one last treat.
It was a ride round the
fire station yard on a
children's fire appliance.
The clever firefighters had
made it specially for their
open day.